To:

From:

Copyright © 2009 Hallmark Licensing, Inc.

Published by Hallmark Books,
a division of Hallmark Cards, Inc.,
Kansas City, MO 64141
Visit us on the Web at www.Hallmark.com.

Art Director: Kevin Swanson
Production Artist: Dan C. Horton

ISBN: 978-1-59530-242-7

BOK1122

Printed and bound in China
MAR12

Shara Tiara
Frog Princess

Written by Chelsea Fogleman • Illustrated by Stacey Lamb

Hallmark
GIFT BOOKS

Shara Tiara was
no ordinary princess.

For starters, she preferred frankfurters to most fancy-pants foods.

No, thanks!

I'm good!

She was never, ever afraid to get dirty.

And, most unprincesslike of all,
Shara liked to do things for herself,
even if it wasn't easy.

One morning, after she brushed her own hair
and made her own bed, Shara set out to play.
But her father was waiting at the door.
"I hope you haven't forgotten the ball," he said.

"Nope," said Shara. "Here it is!"

"Not that kind of ball, my dear! A royal ball . . . a party."

A party! That sounded fun.

"Please go change into your best princess clothes,"
he said. "And whatever you do, do not lose your tiara.
They don't grow on trees, you know!"

Shara groaned. It was not easy having a king for a dad.

While everyone was getting ready for the royal ball, Shara took her baseball outside and practiced her swing.

When she got there, a little frog poked his head out of the water.

"Excuse me, sir," Shara said. "Have you seen my baseball?"

The frog blinked his big white eyes.

"I don't know," he croaked. "What does it look like?"

The ball flew up, up, up, and all the way over the castle wall . . . and right into the moat on the other side.

Shara could not believe her ears.

"It's white with red stitches, of course!" Shara said.
She had seen talking frogs before. But she had never met anyone
who had never seen a baseball.

The little frog searched all around the moat. He found
lots of interesting stuff. But no baseball.

"Let me try one more time," said the frog.
So he did.
And he found it!

The princess was happy!
The frog was happy that the princess was happy!
So they hopped around in a happy little circle.

Now, most princesses would have taken their ball and gone on home. But Shara wanted to thank the little frog who had been so friendly.

"Is there something nice I can do for you?" she asked.

"Well . . ." he whispered (suddenly the frog felt shy). "Do you think I might borrow your crown? Just for a minute?" Like most frogs, he had always dreamed of becoming a prince.

And because she was not your ordinary princess, Shara said, "Sure!"

The little frog jumped from lily pad to lily pad, admiring his reflection in the water.

Shara picked up the baseball and tossed it up and down, up and down. She was having such a wonderful time, but she felt like she was forgetting something . . .

The ball!
She bent down to say good-bye to her friend and get her tiara. But she couldn't get it off the little frog's head.

Shara twisted, tugged, and
turned. But it was no use.

The tiara was STUCK!

"I can't lose another tiara!" said Shara. "And I'm already late for the ball." She sat down on the grass to think. But all she wanted to do was cry.

Sigh...

She looked at the frog wearing the little golden crown. And that made Shara laugh. It made her laugh and laugh until she DID cry. And then . . . she came up with a plan.

But it was not the kind of plan you would expect from an ordinary princess.

It was the silliest, cleverest, most extraordinary plan she'd ever thought up. Shara picked up the little frog and placed him on her head. And with the tiara on the frog and the frog on the princess, they laughed all the way back to the castle.

And they DID have a ball!

And do you know what happened next?

THEY LIVED HOPPILY EVER AFTER!

the end

Did you like
this frog-and-princess
friendship story?

Please send your comments to:
Hallmark Book Feedback
P.O. Box 419034
Mail Drop 215
Kansas City, MO 64141

Or e-mail us at:
booknotes@hallmark.com